JAMES CAM

AVATAR™

HarperFestival is an imprint of HarperCollins Publishers.

James Cameron's Avatar: The Na'vi Quest

Printed in the United States of America.

For information address HarperCollins Children's Books,
a division of HarperCollins Publishers,
10 East 53rd Street, New York, NY 10022.
www.harpercollinschildrens.com

Library of Congress catalog card number: 2009935250
ISBN 978-0-06-180126-6

Book design by John Sazaklis

10 11 12 13 14 WOR 10 9 8 7 6 5 4 3
❖
First Edition

JAMES CAMERON'S

AVATAR™

THE NA'VI QUEST

Based on the motion picture written and directed by James Cameron

Adapted by Nicole Pitesa

HARPER FESTIVAL
An Imprint of HarperCollinsPublishers

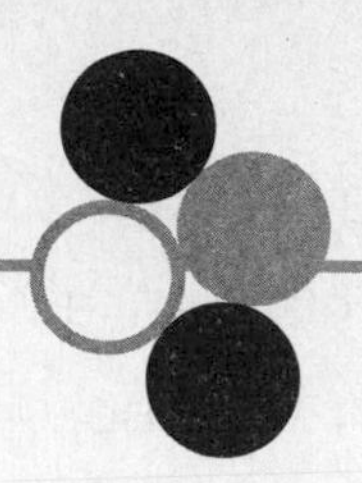

PROLOGUE

EARTH. But this is not the Earth you know. This Earth is no longer lush, green, and full of forests and creatures not yet discovered. Its oceans no longer dance with fish of all shapes and sizes. This is an Earth in the not-so-distant future, where cities of gray have expanded to the horizon and way up high in the sky. Every street is a Times Square display of flashing lights and advertisements viewed by rushing people wearing masks to filter the polluted air. This is a different Earth. This Earth is home to Jake Sully.

All Jake ever wanted in life was something worth fighting for. His strong arms and bad attitude propel him in a wheelchair through the city. Jake's legs haven't walked him anywhere in years. As a former Marine, Jake fought bravely and was crippled in one of the many wars people have waged against one another in this future Earth. And so now, discharged from service, Jake struggles daily to find something that might just make it all worth it.

"Good morning, Sunshine!" Jake opens his eyes, and what feels like a dream begins with a headache and the realization that he has been asleep on a ship traveling through space for five years. He is very far from home. All around him, people are waking up while doctors float around them in zero gravity. Jake is about to set foot on a moon of the planet Polyphemus, called Pandora; if he breathed the air, it would kill him in two minutes flat.

Five years earlier, Jake was stopped on the street by two men who informed him that his twin brother, Tommy, had died while preparing to travel to Pandora. As a scientist, Tommy was hired to join the avatar program, which was designed to make peace with, and learn from, an alien race on Pandora called the Na'vi. They explained to Jake that the program had discovered a way to combine human DNA with Na'vi DNA to grow a hybrid they called an avatar. This avatar would look just like a Na'vi. Jake had no idea what that looked like, but, because he and Tommy were twins and shared the same DNA, Jake could take Tommy's place on the mission and use the avatar created for Tommy. A lot of this was confusing, of course. But what the men said next stopped time for Jake. Through his avatar, Jake could walk again. He could run. He could be the man he once was.

Now, like all of the other scientists, technicians, miners, and security personnel who made the journey, Jake sits through a meeting where he learns that every living thing on Pandora will try to kill him. The man who is talking is Colonel Miles Quaritch, the head of security at Hell's Gate—the human settlement on Pandora. As Colonel Quaritch lectures, Jake can't help but notice that as tough-looking and fit as the colonel is, one entire side of his head and some of his face is scarred by the claws of something that was clearly much bigger than he was.

With the meeting over, Jake learns that his main job in the program is to act as security for the avatar scientists along their various trips and journeys around Pandora. Jake also learns that the entire purpose of Hell's Gate and the avatar program is to obtain one little Pandoran rocklike mineral called *unobtanium* . . . only on Earth it's worth $35 million dollars an ounce.

Jake's head is spinning. But when he meets his avatar for the first time, everything becomes very clear. In a huge tank of water, called an *amnio tank*, floats a body that, if standing, would be ten feet tall. Its skin is the most beautiful two-tone cyan blue imaginable. The skin glimmers in the fluid, and the body twitches like a baby sleeping. The avatar has a long tail, and its body is powerfully muscled and almost humanlike in shape. Its waist is narrow, but its shoulders are wide and strong. Its eyes are closed, though Jake was told that they're gold and catlike. Growing from its head is long black hair that swirls around the body in the tank with a life of its own. When Jake sees its face, he is amazed. Underneath the blue and slightly flattened nose, he could see the features of his brother Tommy's face. And then Jake realizes that it isn't Tommy's face he is seeing. It's his own.

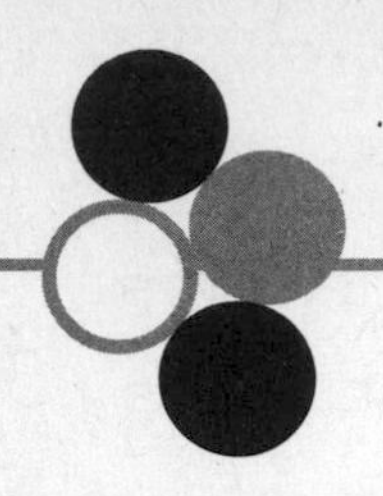

CHAPTER ONE

JAKE WAKES UP AGAIN. Only this time everything is different. Jake's human body is asleep in what is called a *link unit*—a long metal tube full of wiring that connects to his head and chest and allows him to control his avatar with brain waves. But Jake is indeed awake. The hands he lifts in front of his face are long and blue. He stumbles around the room as people who seem so small run around him. His tail moves about, knocking things over, and, unbelievably, he's actually wiggling his toes! Jake is in his avatar body and it's fantastic!

After several days of training and getting used to this new body, Jake is finally ready for work. The helicopter transports Jake and other avatars above lush rain forest full of every shade of green in a crayon box. The air is heavy with mist, and tips of mountains pierce through it. Flocks of some kind of bird in bright rainbow colors fly below them. Jake is struck by the bounty of Pandora, teeming with life.

Once Jake is on the ground, his military training kicks in. He hops off the helicopter with his gun ready. The first thing he notices is the incredible amount of creatures large and small. The trees are thick and so tall that the sky is almost hidden under the leafy canopy. The colors of the forest are unbelievable—not the simple green and brown from the Earth of the past. This forest is an artist's dream of pinks, purples, and blues.

As the group began their first trek through the forest, they are almost immediately greeted by a herd of grazing *sturmbeest*. Jake had learned about them from the books he had been given to read, but to see these buffalo-like creatures with *six* legs up close was breathtaking. Not long after, Jake is startled by a *prolemuris*, a bright yellow, furless kind of monkey that leaps past them from one branch to the next. Jake smiled, feeling like a kid again in this new world. His eyes dart all around him, and each time they pick up on something new.

Jake steps away from the group toward a cluster of fluffy, beautiful plants and gently reaches out his hand to touch the petals when *WHOOP!* It shoots straight down into the ground! He touches another—*WHOOP!* And then he starts touching all of them, laughing—*WHOOP, WHOOP!* When the plants had disappeared, directly in front of him stands an enormous rhinoceros kind of beast whose head is the shape of a hammerhead shark—only it's the size of a house! This is a *hammerhead titanothere* and Jake is most definitely in trouble!

The force of the hammerhead's snort blows back Jake's hair. On its head is what looks like an armor-plated flower—eight petals fan out in neon violets, pinks, and blues. Its body is a deep olive green with gray stripes. It stares at Jake and in a split second charges right for him!

"Hold your ground!" shouts Dr. Grace Augustine, the scientist in charge of the avatar program. The hammerhead thunders down on Jake. Jake turns from Dr. Augustine, screams as loud as he can, and runs right for the beast. The hammerhead stops in its tracks, yelps, turns, and runs away.

"Ha!" Jake starts to laugh and celebrate, still shaking from the rush of fear. Just then, deep within his bones, Jake feels what his ears hear. Behind him there is a deep and very loud growl. Jake freezes every muscle. Before he can take a breath, over his head leaps a pantherlike cat the size of a semitruck and the color of midnight. The monster he knows to be a *thanator* stares down at him with piercing yellow eyes, snarling and revealing long, almost glass teeth. It's angry, and all six of its legs are primed to pounce!

Jake yells to Dr. Augustine, "What about this one? Hold my ground?"

"No, Jake! Run! Definitely run!" Dr. Augustine shouts back.

Jake can feel his heartbeat thundering in his ears as he spins around and sprints through the forest as fast as his new avatar legs can carry him. Operating on pure instinct, he leaps over rocks and crashes through branches and brush. Jake doesn't look back because on his heels is a giant mass of claws and teeth.

In a split second Jake throws himself into the hole created by a nest of tree roots and pulls his gun into position. The thanator slams into the roots with enough force to shake the entire massive tree. Jake squeezes the gun's trigger, but the bullets are useless against the animal. Before he knows what's happening, Jake is thrust into the air. The ground is gone beneath his feet, and the world around him begins to shake. The thanator, which had snatched him up by his backpack, shakes him violently back and forth.

Jake can barely control his arms to reach the levers that release the straps of his backpack. He falls hard but scrambles to his feet and, heart pounding, races toward the sound of a waterfall. In seconds he stands at what feels like the edge of Pandora. Trapped between a long fall and a certain death, Jake takes a deep breath and jumps into the sky!

Struggling to catch his breath under the force of the falls, Jake barely keeps his head above water until he grabs on to a tree limb and drags himself to shore. Still gasping, he looks back toward the cliff and can see the snarling thanator staring down at him. Its roar is heard across the forest.

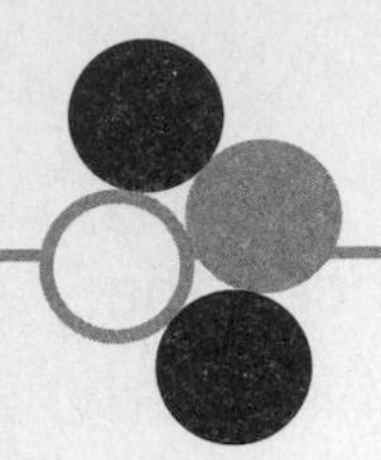

CHAPTER TWO

JAKE CLOSES HIS EYES and the speech Colonel Quaritch gave during orientation replays in his mind. He has to survive this . . . but how? In his pocket Jake finds his knife, and with quick work he fashions a spear from a branch he finds onshore. He looks around himself, having no idea where he is or how he'll get back to the base. He begins to walk. Very carefully.

High in the trees above the forest a pair of golden Na'vi eyes follow Jake's every move. Neytiri, a young Na'vi woman, watches him with a combination of curiosity and anger. Even though Jake looks like a Na'vi, Neytiri can easily see that he is a human-made avatar. Humans! They have already done much to harm the Na'vi people and the forest with their guns and their mining.

Neytiri positions herself, lifts her long bow,

and aims an arrow directly at Jake. She takes a breath and just as she's about to release the arrow, a single light, white dandelion-like seed called a *woodsprite*, or *atokirina* to the Na'vi, drifts through the air, landing on the tip of her arrow. The Na'vi are a very spiritual people, and they believe the woodsprite is a seed from the Great Tree and is connected to Eywa, the Mother of all beings on Pandora. Neytiri focuses on the seed as it lifts from her arrow, floating again. She lowers her weapon.

Night is thick and the sounds of the forest grow louder around Jake. With furious speed he wraps his shirt around the tip of another branch he dips in tree sap. He lights it with his lighter and swings it around himself, revealing that the sounds that have been chasing him came from at least a dozen stealthy, doglike creatures with knife-sharp teeth and glistening black skin striped red. Their six legs allowed them to circle Jake from the ground and silently climb the branches of the trees above him. These are *viperwolves*, and Jake knows it will take a miracle to save him.

Jake waves his torch like a club until he can't hold them off any longer. In a blur of skin and fearsome claws, they attack! Jake swings at one with his torch. Gripping his spear with two hands, he spins around jabbing one after another of the wolves. Jake hears screaming and realizes it's the sound of his own voice as three of the wolves charge him at once, leaping on him with wild jaws snapping! Knocked to the ground, Jake kicks his legs and swings his spear wildly.

One set of jaws clamps down on his spear, tearing it from his hands. Now all that separates Jake from the teeth in front of his face are his own two hands.

He pushes against the beast with all of his might when suddenly it goes limp. Jake rolls the beast to the ground—a long arrow coming from its chest. He looks up and suddenly everything around him moves in slow motion.

A flash of blue jumps from a tree above him. Viperwolves begin to fall around him. In an instant the remaining wolves have disappeared, whimpering into the forest. In front of Jake is a slim, muscled Na'vi woman who stands tall and elegant. Her tail swishes as she crouches over a fallen viperwolf, and Jake realizes this Na'vi is beautiful. She removes her arrows from the wolves that had died, all the while whispering in a language Jake had struggled to learn and pronounce.

Neytiri grabs Jake's still-lit torch and tosses it into the river. "Wait! Don't!" Jake cries out. Neytiri charges up to Jake and in English shouts, "This is your fault! They did not need to die!"

"Wait, they attacked *me*! How am I the bad guy?" Jake asks. He doesn't understand how she can be angry.

"You should not come here. You only make

problems! You are like a baby, making noise!" Neytiri responds.

"Okay, fine, you love your little forest friends. So why not just let them kill me?" he retorts.

Neytiri thinks for a moment, then quietly says, "You have a strong heart. No fear." She pauses. "But stupid! Like child," she adds.

Jake laughs a bit nervously. He's lost and alone, and he needs her help.

"If I'm so stupid, maybe you should teach me."

Frustrated, Neytiri turns and makes her way through the forest at a quick pace. Jake looks around and realizes that without the torch, the forest comes alive. The plants and trees actually glow! There are clear mushrooms and ferns colored blue-green and purple. Even the moss on the trees glows bright yellow. To his amazement, Jake realizes he can see perfectly in the dark.

Jake chases after Neytiri, struggling to keep up. His new body is strong, but he's clumsy and slow. They climb high and low—over vast ravines and steep cliffs. They're sprinting across a large tree-trunk bridge over a ravine when Jake gets caught on a vine and loses his footing. Neytiri spins back and nimbly catches him by the arm just in time.

"Go back," she says. Her eyes are serious.

"I need your help," Jake pleads.

"No! Go back!"

Neytiri takes a step back, still holding on to Jake's arm, as dozens of woodsprites float down from the canopy above. They glow and pulse, moving through the air toward Jake, circling him and landing on his chest and arms. They cover his body in a swirl of white light as Neytiri gasps.

"What are they?" Jake asks, and begins to swat them away.

"No!" Neytiri shouts. "These are seeds of the Great Tree." Her eyes are wide with surprise.

In an instant, the woodsprites float off of Jake and back into the trees.

Neytiri looks long and hard at Jake. "Come!" she says, taking hold of Jake's hand, leading him through the forest.

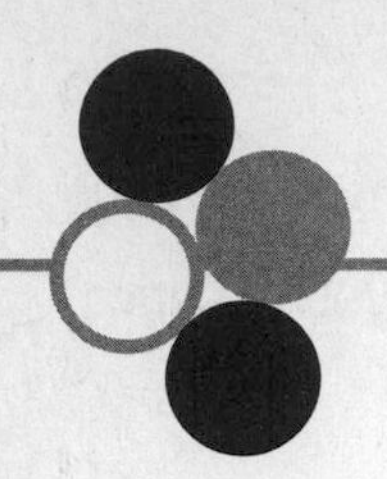

CHAPTER THREE

JAKE STAYS AS CLOSE to Neytiri's heels as he can as they travel deeper into the thick forest. It's hard for Jake to stay focused—his attention is distracted by the beauty around him. Every single thing glows and reacts to their bodies. Even the moss beneath their feet leaves rings of light in the shapes of their footfalls as they pass. As scared as he is, Jake can't help smiling.

Jake trips over a root and lands hard in the undergrowth below. But when he begins to untangle himself, he sees he didn't trip at all. Wrapped tightly around his feet is the Na'vi rope-weapon he'd read about—a bola. A storm of Na'vi warriors riding what look like exotic and powerful animals called *direhorses* thunder down and surround them.

"Tsu'tey!" Neytiri shouts angrily at the group's

leader as he jumps from his direhorse. Jake realizes Neytiri knows these Na'vi, but somehow that isn't very comforting.

"These demons are forbidden here!" Tsu'tey shouts. He is tall and powerful with well-defined muscles and a face that would scare a child. "I will kill this one as a lesson to the others!" The circle of warriors around Jake tightens as Tsu'tey draws his bow.

"No!" Neytiri shouts, jumping between Tsu'tey and Jake. "He is my captive and there was a sign from Eywa. It is for the *tsahik* to decide what will be done with him, not you!"

Tsu'tey clenches his jaw. He jumps back onto his direhorse and commands the others to bring Jake. Not long after, the forest clears and before Jake stands a tree towering above him like a skyscraper. Its foundation is a maze of root pillars. This tree, which the Na'vi call *Hometree*, is one of Pandora's Great Trees, and home to Neytiri's clan, the *Omaticaya*.

The group ride into the base of the tree, and villagers began to gather, whispering and curious. Firelight flickers against the shadows on the walls, and insects glow from glasslike containers suspended from the vast root system. Jake's gaze climbs high up the inside of the tree until it rests on what must be the village totem. On its top is a huge skull of a creature Jake hopes is extinct.

Its nose is long and pointed, and its mouth is full of long, sharp teeth.

"Why do you bring this creature here?" The booming voice belongs to an older Na'vi wearing a large necklace of thanator claws. Jake can tell he is the clan's leader. He is angry and Jake realizes that he is talking about him!

"I was going to kill him," replies Neytiri. "But there was a sign from Eywa."

She was going to kill me? Jake is getting more uncomfortable by the minute. In the fast-paced Na'vi language, Neytiri tells the older Na'vi about the atokirinas that had touched Jake.

"What is going on?" Jake whispers to Neytiri.

"My father is deciding whether or not to kill you," she replies.

"Your *father*?" Jake's surprised. He steps forward, stretching his hand out to Eytukan. "Nice to meet you, sir—"

In a flash, warriors rush over to Jake—knocking him back and grabbing him from all directions.

"Step back!" comes a commanding voice that

makes everyone in the room stop and listen. Even Jake holds his breath. From the upper level of Hometree, a small, older Na'vi woman descends the stairs. She's adorned in a robe that makes her look royal. As if reading his mind, Neytiri says in a low voice, "That is Mother, Mo'at. She is tsahik—the one who interprets the will of Eywa." Jake understood this to be some sort of Mother Nature.

The villagers bow their heads as Mo'at approaches. "I will look at this alien," she says. Her voice is deep and her English is heavily accented. She walks within inches of Jake and demands, "What are you called?"

"Jake Sully," Jake replies. "I came here to learn."

Mo'at circles Jake, inspecting every inch of him, smelling him, picking up his *queue*—the long, black hair that allows the Na'vi to connect physically to the creatures of Pandora.

"We have tried to teach other *skypeople*," Mo'at says, referring to humans and avatars. "It is hard to fill a cup which is already full."

"Trust me," Jake says. "My cup is empty, I'm no scientist."

"Are you not?" Mo'at is curious, cocking her head to the side and looking at Jake from a new angle. "If you're not a scientist, what are you?"

Jake is nervous now. "I *was* a warrior."

Eytukan and Mo'at look at each other. Jake has their attention. They've never met a warrior *dreamwalker*. Only scientists walked in avatar bodies. In silence, they made a decision. The humans had been nothing but a stain on Pandora, but perhaps they can study this warrior and learn how to rid themselves of the stain and restore peace.

Mo'at turns to Neytiri. "You will teach this Jakesully our ways—to speak and walk as we do."

"No, I —" Neytiri begins to protest.

"It is decided!" And with that, there is no discussion. Even Jake knows that. Mo'at shifts her focus to Jake.

"My daughter will teach you our ways. Learn well, Jakesully." Neytiri roughly grabs Jake by the arm and pulls him away.

"Neytiri will test this warrior," Mo'at whispers to Eytukan. "He may learn nothing, but we will learn much."

Neytiri shoves a plate of food in front of Jake. He picks up a slippery white bit of something and tosses it in his mouth. It pops on his tongue and tastes divine—the perfect blend of salt and something else he can't quite put his finger on.

"These rock! What are they?" he asks Neytiri.

"*Teylu*," she answers, annoyed and not looking at him. "You call them beetle larvae."

Jake coughs, spits out what's left in his mouth, and wipes his face furiously. He sees that Neytiri has a grin on her face, and he realizes that to fit in and to learn, he is going to have to try a lot of new things. He puts his hand on the plate again and shoves a big handful of the teylu into his mouth.

"I say she will kill him," Tsu'tey says to Mo'at and Eytukan, watching impatiently as Neytiri begins her lessons with Jake.

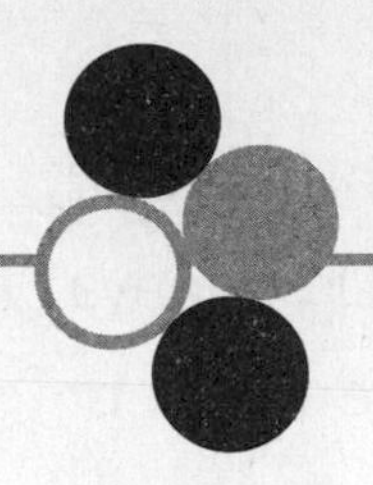

CHAPTER FOUR

JAKE OPENS HIS EYES. He's not in the beautiful, woven hammock he had fallen asleep in. Gone is the natural, earthy beauty of Hometree with the quiet sounds of Na'vi around him, sleeping. In front of him is a med tech calling medical stats and shining a light into his eyes. He's hooked up to cables, and his legs are just as useless as he remembers. Questions fire at him from Dr. Augustine and the other scientists, as well as the security personnel. Where was the avatar? What happened to him? Was the avatar safe? Jake explains to wide eyes and shocked faces all the details of the thanator chase and what came after. Everyone is thrilled that he's with the Omaticaya clan. For years the avatar program tried to gain the trust of the Omaticaya, but all the damage the humans had caused made that impossible.

Dr. Augustine is excited at the possibilities and all they can potentially learn from the Omaticaya about the plants, the animals, and the heart of Pandora.

Colonel Quaritch has other plans. He's quick to pull Jake aside and explain that Hometree is located directly on top of a huge deposit of unobtanium the human crews are ready to mine. He's impressed by Jake's military background and wants Jake to report back to him as much information about the clan and the area around Hometree as possible. It's the colonel's hope that Jake will persuade the Omaticaya to move to a new location, and, if not, he will use the information he'll gather from Jake to simply force them out. In exchange for his help, the colonel promises Jake he will arrange for him to have the use of his legs restored once he returns to Earth. Jake understands the colonel's position, and surgery is all he needs to sell him on the plan. Their agreement and Jake's mission will be their little secret.

Jake opens his eyes again. But now, streams

of sunlight pour into Hometree from its cathedral-like canopy. He stretches his avatar body and realizes that he's the last one up. The Na'vi around him are busy weaving, cleaning fish, whispering, and singing. Children run and play. Jake's early morning smile fades, however, when he sees Neytiri approaching him on a direhorse. Behind her is an old and swaybacked direhorse. It is obvious that his first day of learning the ways of the Na'vi is going to be a long one.

The direhorses have long, regal snouts and thin ears that are pointed back. Their long necks and backs are covered in gray stripes, accented with bright red and blue. In an open space beyond Hometree, Neytiri holds the direhorse's nose ring as Jake clumsily climbs into the saddle. Jake knows he has to *bond* with the animal—whatever that means. Prompted by Neytiri, Jake takes one of the direhorse's antennae and brings it to the tip of his queue. The two weave together and Jake's entire body shivers. His mouth falls open and everything tingles as the direhorse honks and shakes.

Neytiri touches where the two are connected.

"This is *shahaylu*," she tells Jake. "The Bond. Feel her heartbeat, her breath. Feel her strong legs."

Jake closes his eyes and actually *feels* the direhorse.

"You may tell her what to do," Neytiri tells him. She touches her head, indicating he can do this with his mind. "For now, say where to go."

Bracing himself, Jake says, "Forward."

The direhorse launches forward! Jake bounces uncontrollably, flailing about, and flies from the horse to the ground. He laughs painfully and slowly stands up as Neytiri leads the horse back to him. Jake hobbles over to his mount.

"Again," Neytiri commands.

Jake tries again. And again, and again. He's sure he's spending more time on the ground than in the saddle. Each time he falls, Neytiri issues the same command, "Again."

Thrown from the horse for what has to be the fifteenth time, Jake pushes himself to a kneeling position. Above him stands Tsu'tey and another Na'vi male on direhorses.

"You should go away," Tsu'tey says to Jake.

"I knew this guy could speak English," Jake replies with a slight smile to no one in particular.

Tsu'tey turns to Neytiri. "This alien will learn nothing. A rock sees more." With that, he and his companion ride into the forest with skill and speed.

Neytiri sighs heavily, looks at Jake, and says, "Again."

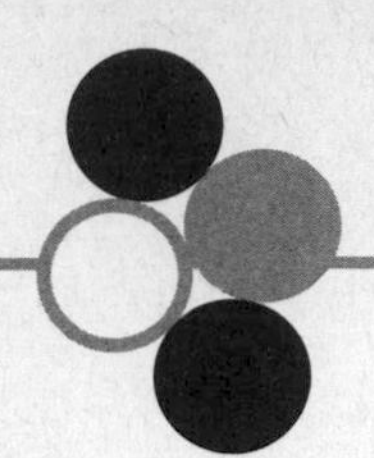

CHAPTER FIVE

LEARNING TO RIDE A DIREHORSE is only the beginning of Jake's training. In the days that follow he increases his Na'vi vocabulary and learns how to shoot arrows with a bow and to fish with a spear. Jake is also paying close attention to the layout of Hometree and reporting back to Colonel Quaritch with maps and detailed descriptions.

Every day brings new lessons, and today is no different. Just after waking, Neytiri orders Jake to follow her higher into Hometree. As usual, Jake struggles to keep up with her quick, silent movements. She effortlessly leaps from branch to branch while Jake slowly climbs. When they reach the top, they are so high up that the Na'vi below them look like ants.

Neytiri guides Jake to a huge branch, giving them a view of the entire horizon. Jake gazes

across the vast expanse of forest that covers Pandora's surface. In the distance, towering high above the canopy, Jake sees other Great Trees much like Hometree. There are tremendous mountains that—*What?* He can't believe it—the mountains are *floating* above the ground! Braided and twisted tree roots dangle from the mountains' craggy bottoms, tying them to the surface below, as waterfalls spray mist over the green forest.

Snapping Jake from his trance, Neytiri walks toward a structure that looks like a web of thick woven fiber. Jake follows her, noticing that clinging to the web are dark shapes that rustle and stir. A little scared of what might be inside, Jake stays close to his teacher.

Neytiri emits a series of trills and clicks, and out of the dark appears a huge birdlike creature with massive wings, claws, and teeth. Jake jumps back when with a leathery *FWHOOP*, it takes to the sky and lands on the branch in front of them.

"Holy cow!" Jake exclaimed. This was no direhorse. This was a huge mountain *banshee*. It walks on four legs, its folded wings jutting out from its shoulders and its knees. Black stripes mixed with yellow and blue cover its skin while beneath its chin, a red dewlap lies folded.

"Do not look her in the eye," Neytiri warns. The beast grabs a piece of meat from Neytiri's hand and gulps it down. She steps closer to the banshee, talking to her and stoking her neck. As Neytiri pets her friend, the banshee lets out an ear-piercing shriek, followed by the shrieks of the other banshees still hidden from view. The sky is full of the sound.

Neytiri connects her queue to the banshee's antenna. The banshee shivers and stretches her wings. The sheer power of the animal is amazing. Neytiri returns her focus to Jake.

"*Ikran* is not horse. Once *shahaylu* is made, ikran will fly with only one Hunter in the whole life." She climbs onto its back.

"To become *Taronyu*—Hunter—you must choose your own ikran. And he must choose you."

"When?" Jake asks.

"When you are ready," she replies. The banshee's enormous wings open, and she lifts off with Neytiri saddled on her back. The hunter and her mount fly over the forest canopy. The banshee's four wings spread like a butterfly's as she soars.

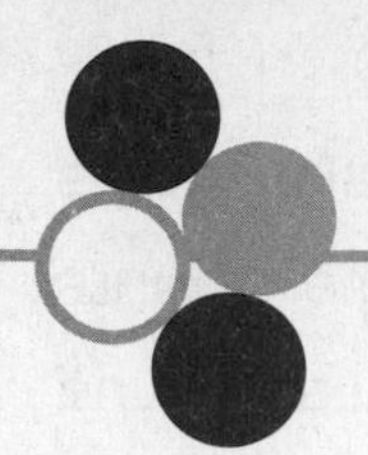

CHAPTER SIX

THE DAYS BLUR TOGETHER FOR JAKE. He's spending every waking moment learning, and less and less time on his mission for Colonel Quaritch. The colonel is starting to hound Jake for information, while Jake stalls as much as possible. For the first time in a long time, Jake feels his heart and begins to question whether Quaritch's mission is right. He is feeling a connection to the Omaticaya and no one is more surprised than he is.

Each week brings more strength to Jake's muscles and more agility to his limbs. He speaks entire Na'vi sentences and can now handle their weapons. Neytiri is gaining confidence in him and testing him further. She takes Jake running in the forest and teaches him how to move through it by leaping from branches and leaves without ever touching the ground. Jake learns to track animals through scents in the air, prints in the mud, and the way sound moves around him in the trees. And then, Neytiri teaches him to hunt.

On their first pursuit, Jake and Neytiri stalk in silence, focusing on a large *hexapede* feeding on leaves. The bearded animal with unique, colored horns is unaware it's being watched. With Neytiri's help, Jake expertly aims an arrow at the blue-furred animal, following its moves through the trees. Jake lowers his bow. Although he's learning the Omaticaya ways, Neytiri told him the forest had not yet given him permission to take a life. Jake is beginning to learn from Neytiri that all animals on Pandora are linked together through natural energy. Before he can take a life, he has to understand that entirely.

As night falls, they walk through the forest. Jake's avatar eyes see clearly as Neytiri leads him to a glimmering pool. There they fish from a canoe, as below them, huge anemone-like swimming creatures light up the water. Jake spears one and lets out a cheer. He is definitely getting the hang of this.

Later, they enter a clearing of enormous ferns. Neytiri puts her finger to her lips, signaling Jake to move quietly. She points in the direction of a large, flat leaf on which is perched a small lizardlike creature. Jake moves in for a closer look and *WHOOSH!*—the lizard opens glowing wings that spin like a helicopter propeller. Neytiri lets out a gleeful cry and jumps into the ferns. Dozens of fan lizards light up the air, spinning like Frisbees.

More days pass and Jake feels at home in his avatar body. His life with the Omaticaya is becoming reality, while his human life at the base becomes the dream. He realizes that he and Neytiri have actually become friends and their lessons are something they both look forward to.

The next morning, Neytiri takes Jake hunting again. And this time, as Jake aims his arrow at a hexapede grazing, Neytiri nods when the time is right. Jake releases the arrow in silence and the

hexapede falls. Jake's heart is beating fast, and as he stands over the fallen animal, he whispers in Na'vi, "I see you, brother, and thank you. Your spirit goes with Eywa, your body stays behind to become part of the people." Neytiri watches Jake with proud eyes, and nods.

CHAPTER SEVEN

JAKE'S REPORTS TO COLONEL QUARITCH become less frequent. Each day with Neytiri and the Omaticaya take him further away from Earth. He is focused on learning all he can from Neytiri and proving to the clan that he can be one of them.

Back at Hell's Gate, Jake's human body is getting weak. He rarely eats and sleeps. His once short military haircut is now long and shaggy, accented by a thick beard across his face. Dr. Augustine tries to remind him that his experiences in his avatar body are a dream that requires millions of dollars to sustain, and that his crippled human body is his reality—as hard as that is to believe now. But for the first time in a long time, Jake has a purpose. And he's going to see this through.

Tsu'tey leads Jake and two teenaged hunters through the forest and up a steep mountain trail on direhorses. A feeling of pride tickles Jake's chest, as he has no trouble keeping up with them. Jake and the others are riding to a test that will bring him closer to the Omaticaya. He's nervous that Tsu'tey's in charge.

The direhorses halt at a cliff opening to a misty canyon. Jake sees they are high above the forest below. Huge boulders of weightless unobtanium are trapped midair by giant, vinelike tree systems. Trees shoot out from the rock, tethered by their roots, which grow straight through the rock and down into the ground like beanstalks. They soar like hot-air balloons on strings and are as high as the eyes can see, piercing through the clouds. A loud roar echoes as the hunters watch. One of the rock formations brushes against another, sending huge amounts of dirt and rock down to the surface below. This is *Iknimaya*, or "Stairway to Heaven." Each young Na'vi warrior must pass this test before becoming an adult. The climb itself represented just one half of the test. The second awaited them at the top.

Jake stands back, trying to remember all Neytiri has taught him. He can do this. He knows it. He looks at Tsu'tey and asks, "We doing this?" And as Tsu'tey nods, Jake runs to the edge of the cliff and leaps into the air with outstretched arms. His hands grasp roots and Jake's body begins to climb.

The ache in Jake's muscles tell him he's climbed far and high. He looks down. The direhorses are nothing but specks on the cliff below! Jake continues climbing, breaking off pieces of rock as he moves. But instead of falling down, the pieces float up!

They reach the upper branches of a strange tree and find the bottom of a giant mountain called Mons Veritas. Vines flow down from its base and brush past them as the mountain moves. Other floating islands hover around the giant rock. One by one, the hunters grab the vines, lifting themselves up and onto one of the islands. Jake looks down and all he sees now is nothingness. His heart beats loudly in his ears, but he remains focused on the task ahead and feels secure in his training.

At last their feet touch down on the top of Mons Veritas. Jake ducks his head as huge mountain banshees circle the air above them. They dart in and out of shafts of sunlight and around the waterfalls that pour not into rivers, but dissolve into the sky. The mountain banshees are much bigger than forest banshees. They are a brilliant blue and green—and scary. Jake is aware that with bigger size comes bigger teeth!

Tsu'tey leads the hunters along steep and narrow cliffs. Jake is extremely careful as he follows—one false move and he would topple into the air. They come to a sudden stop. Jake feels a giant *SWOOSH* of air and hears a loud, leatherlike *SNAP!* He looks up. Landing on the cliff's edge in front of them is Neytiri and her ikran. Jake is very relieved. Neytiri smiles at Jake and jumps from the creature, joining the small group as they emerge onto the face of a cliff.

In front of them are *hundreds* of ikran on the rock face, digging in with their long foreclaws. Some perch on ledges while others take flight.

"Jakesully will go first," Tsu'tey announces to the group. He smiles at Jake. It's clear that Tsu'tey expects Jake to fail—and is looking forward to it. Neytiri takes Jake by the hand and leads him closer to the banshees.

"Now you must choose your ikran," she says. "This you must feel, inside." Her hand rests on his heart. "If he also chooses you, move quick, like I showed—you will only have one chance."

"How will I know if he chooses me?" Jake asks.

"He will try to kill you," Neytiri answers.

"Outstanding," Jake murmurs. Neytiri backs away to join the others and watch. Jake is on his own, and he carefully approaches the banshees. They turn to him, hissing. Some back away; others simply ignore him. Jake unrolls his bola so it's ready.

Jake turns and there, towering above him, one banshee stares him directly in the eyes and hisses. Jake instantly begins swinging his bola—this is the *one*. He feels it in his chest just like Neytiri said he would.

"Let's dance," Jake says to the creature. The ikran's teeth are deadly and bared. Jake sprints right for him and releases his bola at just the right moment. The weight of the bola snaps the beast's jaws shut, wrapping around his mouth twice. Jake launches himself onto the back of the angry ikran. His claws rake Jake, but Jake's arms wrap around the neck. The ikran is shaking him about and Jake feels like he's riding a bull at a rodeo without a saddle. He knows he has to make the bond quickly. It's only a matter of seconds before the beast shakes Jake loose and the bola loosens around the banshee's jaws. He reaches for the creature's long, whipping antenna but the ikran slams him and sends him sliding through the dirt and over the cliff's edge!

Jake grabs onto the roots just below the edge and pulls himself back up. Not even taking a second to catch his breath, Jake throws himself onto the beast's bucking back. Neytiri is shouting at Jake, "Shahaylu, Jake! You must make the bond!" Jake can hear Tsu'tey laughing and telling the other hunters that Jake is going to die. But Jake is not finished yet!

Struggling to right himself on the ikran's back, Jake pulls his queue forward and snatches the creature's antenna. And with not a second to spare, the two are linked. Almost immediately the beast is still. Jake sucks in deep mouthfuls of air and tries to calm himself.

"That's right," Jake says to the ikran. "You're mine."

Neytiri runs toward him, smiling. "First flight seals the bond. You cannot wait!"

Jake settles himself on the creature's back, still breathing hard, heart racing. He takes a firm hold at the base of each of the ikran's two antennae.

"Heeyah!" he shouts, instructing the beast to take off.

The ikran's wings open and beat. They shoot off the cliff, diving into the open air. Both Jake and the ikran scream as they spiral out of control through the sky. They bash against rocks and streak through a waterfall before Jake realizes he must focus and guide the creature. But the ikran was screeching so much that he couldn't think.

"Shut up!" Jake shouts in frustration. "Level out! Fly straight!" he commands. The creature calms and does exactly as instructed, surprising Jake. His training was coming back to him now—but *this* was no direhorse!

"Bank left," he commands the animal with his mind. And they do just that, as the animal's wings beat strong and smooth. Jake feels he was born to do this! Neytiri joins him on her ikran and Jake follows her, the student again. Where Neytiri flies confidently and evenly, Jake's ikran still wobbles and dips as he adjusts to his rider.

Now, Neytiri can show Jake Pandora from the sky. They swoop between trees and behind waterfalls. They skim close to cliffs and burst through clouds. Jake glides above Pandora, dives down sharply and hugs his body close to the power of his ikran. "Woo-hoo!" he shouts.

Over the next days, Neytiri helps Jake to perfect the art of flying. On the ground she teaches him basic flight safety. In the air she teaches him acrobatics. Jake can't get enough! Tsu'tey and his young riders also join Jake and Neytiri on their flights. As a group, they fly in tight patterns and at high speeds.

Jake hones his skills as he and Neytiri chase each other through the sky, darting behind clouds and racing past each other. Just when Jake thinks he's caught up with Neytiri, she smiles and dives away, making him chase her again. If there is a heaven, Jake is sure this is it.

Jake's bond with his ikran is strong. When they aren't flying, Jake spends time with him, feeding and petting him.

Acrobatics, though fun, are training for the reason the Na'vi ride the ikran—to hunt from the air. Neytiri shows Jake how to perch, how to survey the forest below, and how to strike without casting a shadow. Neytiri is teaching Jake to steady himself on the ikran's back with only his legs—freeing his arms to use his bow and arrow—when the two of them are covered by a huge shadow! Neytiri shouts in warning and Jake looks up to see a giant, flame-red *leonopteryx* diving straight for him! The enormous beast is easily twice the size of Jake's ikran and has a blue-crested head and red-yellow-and-black-striped body. Jake needs to think—fast!

Jake rolls his banshee and dives into the forest. He shears in and out of trees while behind him he hears the beast's roar. In a panic, Jake makes a sharp turn right through the gap between two huge trunks. The giant creature can't go any farther, but Jake continues flying, burying himself deeper into the forest. The leonopteryx screeches and soars back above the forest, its fangs glistening in the sun. Its cry echoes across the landscape as Neytiri catches up to Jake, wearing an expression of shock that Jake survived.

Jake had now seen in person the creature behind the skull on the totem at Hometree—the giant leonopteryx—Toruk, as the people call it. It is also called the Last Shadow, as its shadow is the last thing you'll ever see.

Jake is becoming one of the Omaticaya now. His expert flying makes him an important member when he hunts with the group. It's Jake's arrow that takes down the huge sturmbeest on

hunting trips. It's Jake who is honored at the hunting celebrations, along with all of the other brave hunters. And it's Jake whose leonopteryx story hushes crowds and makes children listen with eyes wide with fear and wonder.

"I did not think a skyperson could be brave," Tsu'tey says to Jake as he nods at him. But before Jake can answer, Neytiri grabs him, pulling him to the center of the circle where they dance and celebrate. He loves being with Neytiri. He feels alive. And as he looks around him, he feels at home. But there's just one more test.

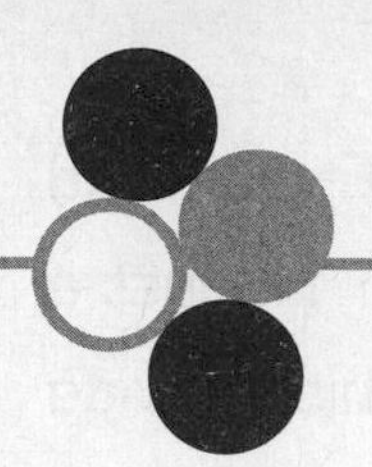

CHAPTER EIGHT

COLONEL QUARITCH continues to pressure Jake. Quaritch had told Jake he had three months to move the Omaticaya from Hometree before he forces them out, and that time is now. Jake pleads with the colonel, explaining that he has just one more test—the Dream Hunt, and if he passes it, he will be one of the people. And then they will listen to him.

Jake knows in his heart that to betray the Omaticaya is wrong. But he feels he can somehow reason with them and with Quaritch once he passes the final test. He needs help and sits down with Dr. Augustine, who has become almost a mother to Jake in the last few months, caring for him and forcing his human body to eat, even when he didn't want to. She has seen the change in Jake and realizes that he's not at all the same person who wheeled himself and his dark cloud of a personality into her lab just a few months before. It's because of this change that, when Jake tells her of his secret work with Quaritch, she forgives him and agrees that they need to do all they can to prevent an attack upon Hometree.

Jake finally knows what it means to believe in something. And more than anything he has ever wanted in his life, he wants to complete the Dream Hunt and *become* Na'vi.

"You can never be one of them, Jake." Dr. Augustine looks at him sadly.

"It's the last door—I'm going through it. You can help me or get out of the way," Jake replies.

"Will you listen to me?" Dr. Augustine tries to reason with Jake. "Sometimes the Na'vi themselves die in these vision quests! We have no idea what it will do in an avatar brain."

"I have to go all the way and become one of them." Jake closes his eyes in his link unit once again and opens them in Hometree. He walks down a spiral staircase toward the lowest level of Hometree, where a group of elders and celebrated hunters is waiting for him. A huge drum beats as Mo'at comes forward, chanting in a low voice and purifying Jake with the smoke of burning herbs.

Mo'at carefully unwraps a piece of wood covered with darkened holes. From one of the holes she pulls a glowing purple worm, places it on Jake's tongue, and says, "Oh, wise worm, eater of the Sacred Tree, bless this worthy Hunter with true vision." Mo'at makes a chewing motion with her jaw and Jake follows her lead and bites down on the worm, which tastes much like teylu. Jake swallows, waiting for what will come next.

Jake watches as Eytukan approaches him with a clay jar. From it, Eytukan pulls a wriggling black arachnid and walks to Jake, staring directly in Jake's eyes. Eytukan places the creature onto Jake's neck, where his veins can be seen beating in anticipation. Jake winces as he feels the burn of its sting. He knows that the worm and this poison will start the Dream Hunt and bring to him his spirit animal, but he is not sure exactly how.

Jake looks around at the elders and their faces change into strange shapes. Jake brings his hands up, watching as his body, the ground, and the entire circle of Na'vi disappear. The poisons had taken effect, and out of the darkness around him emerges a ring of enormous glowing trees. He is flying above them. The entire forest of Pandora is aflame and its beauty is in ruin. Jake looks back at his body. His fingers stretch into vines and his legs become roots, spreading out across the ground and connecting to the roots of the ring of trees that surrounds him. And now, suddenly, he's standing on the floating cliff of Mons Veritas where the Last Shadow flew above him. Time speeds up as clouds roll past. The burned forest is lifeless beneath him. Jake is flying above the surface of the future Pandora. He sees the great shadow beneath him and realizes that he is the one casting it! *He* is the great leonopteryx, flying high. He lets out a piercing shriek across the arc of the planet.

In the circle, the elders watch as Jake's avatar shakes and struggles through his vision. He has been wriggling on the ground, his eyes rolling back in his head. Neytiri and the others are happy when his eyes open. He rolls to one side, gasping for air with sweat pouring down his body. He feels as if he's been run over by a truck. He sits up and looks around the room.

"It is finished," Mo'at announces, looking at Jake.

"Did your spirit animal come?" Eytukan asks Jake. Looking from Mo'at to Eytukan and the others, Jake tries to form words to describe what he had just been through, but he can't. How can he possibly tell them of the burning forest and that his spirit animal is the great *Toruk*? Mo'at approaches Jake, placing her fingers against his face, and peers into his very soul.

"Something has come," she says. Stepping back, she motions to him to stand. Jake struggles to his feet and walks out of the circle.

Eytukan leads Jake outside, where the entire clan is waiting. He touches Jake's chest. "You are now a son of the Omaticaya. You are part of the people."

A great rush of Na'vi press forward to congratulate Jake. Jake's chest is so full, he feels he'll burst with pride. Over the last three months he thought he was struggling to prove himself worthy to Neytiri and to Tsu'tey. But now he realizes that he was trying to prove his worth to himself. He had done it! Now he is focused and knows he has to do all he can to not only save the Omaticaya and Hometree from the humans, but to save all of Pandora—and himself. He takes a hold of Neytiri's hand.

Jake had finally found something worth fighting for.